BEING FRIENDS WITH DRAGONS

Written by **KATHERINE LOCKE**

Illustrated by **DIANE EWEN**

RP|KIDS
PHILADELPHIA

TO ALL THE DRAGONS IN MY LIFE, AND THOSE
WHO LOVE ME EVEN WHEN I AM A DRAGON
– K.L.

FOR M.G.E AND DRAGON LOVERS EVERYWHERE
– D.E.

Running Press Kids
Hachette Book Group
1290 Avenue of the Americas, New York, NY 10104
www.runningpress.com/rpkids
@RP_Kids

Printed in China

First Edition: February 2022

Published by Running Press Kids, an imprint of Perseus Books, LLC, a subsidiary of
Hachette Book Group, Inc. The Running Press Kids name and logo is a trademark
of the Hachette Book Group.

The Hachette Speakers Bureau provides a wide range of authors for speaking events.
To find out more, go to www.hachettespeakersbureau.com or call (866) 376-6591.

The publisher is not responsible for websites (or their content)
that are not owned by the publisher.

Print book cover and interior design by Marissa Raybuck.

Library of Congress Control Number: 2020940705

ISBNs: 978-0-7624-7324-3 (hardcover), 978-0-7624-7368-7 (ebook),
978-0-7624-7322-9 (ebook), 978-0-7624-7369-4 (ebook)

APS

10 9 8 7 6 5 4 3 2 1

Dragons can be great friends!

Dragons always know
the best games.

They are champions at hide-and-seek
because they can sniff out any hiding spot!

Dragons love to go camping.
They have an excellent
sense of direction, and they
toast the perfect marshmallows!

Dragons are very
good at slides,

and not so good
at monkey bars.

And they'll always push you on the swings.

Dragons love to go to the shore
and collect sparkly rocks and seashells.
But they are *not* fans of the surf.

Dragons are very tall,
so they can always
reach the top shelf.

And dragons have sharp claws,
so they can help scratch your back.

They are very sneaky, too,
so they can open the
cookie jar undetected!

Dragons also love to cook!
They have lots of favorite recipes.
You might even like some of them.

But sometimes dragons can *forget* to be good friends.

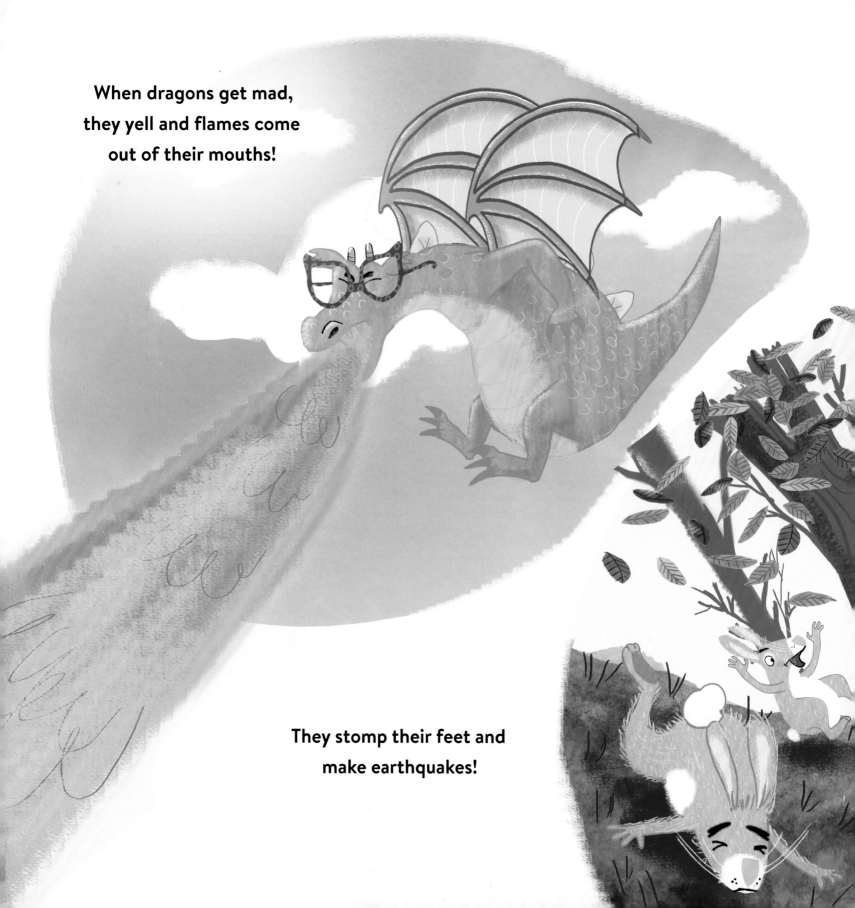

When dragons get mad, they yell and flames come out of their mouths!

They stomp their feet and make earthquakes!

They cross their arms and make thunderstorms!

Dragons don't always listen
to their friends.

And dragons aren't
always good at sharing.

They always want to play
their games and not yours.

When your dragon doesn't want to share,
and when your dragon doesn't listen to you,
and when your dragon won't play your games,

you might yell and
stomp your feet!

You might sulk and
cross your arms!

You might cry and
say mean things!

It can be hard beings friends with dragons.

But dragons know just what to do when this happens.

(Let's face it: Dragons know a dragon when they see one.)

Dragons say they're sorry,
and dragons help clean up any
mess they have made.

Bin
It

Dragons remind each other that next time,
they can take a deep breath and
calm themselves before they get mad.

Dragons remind each other to share,
to take turns, and to say please and thank you.

And if your dragon isn't listening,
use your dragon voice—calm but loud—
so your dragon hears you and remembers.

Being friends with a dragon
isn't always easy.
But it is a lot of fun!

With some perfectly toasted marshmallows
and some very sparkly rocks,

a favorite recipe and a game
of hide-and-seek . . .

you and your dragon can stay
best friends—forever.

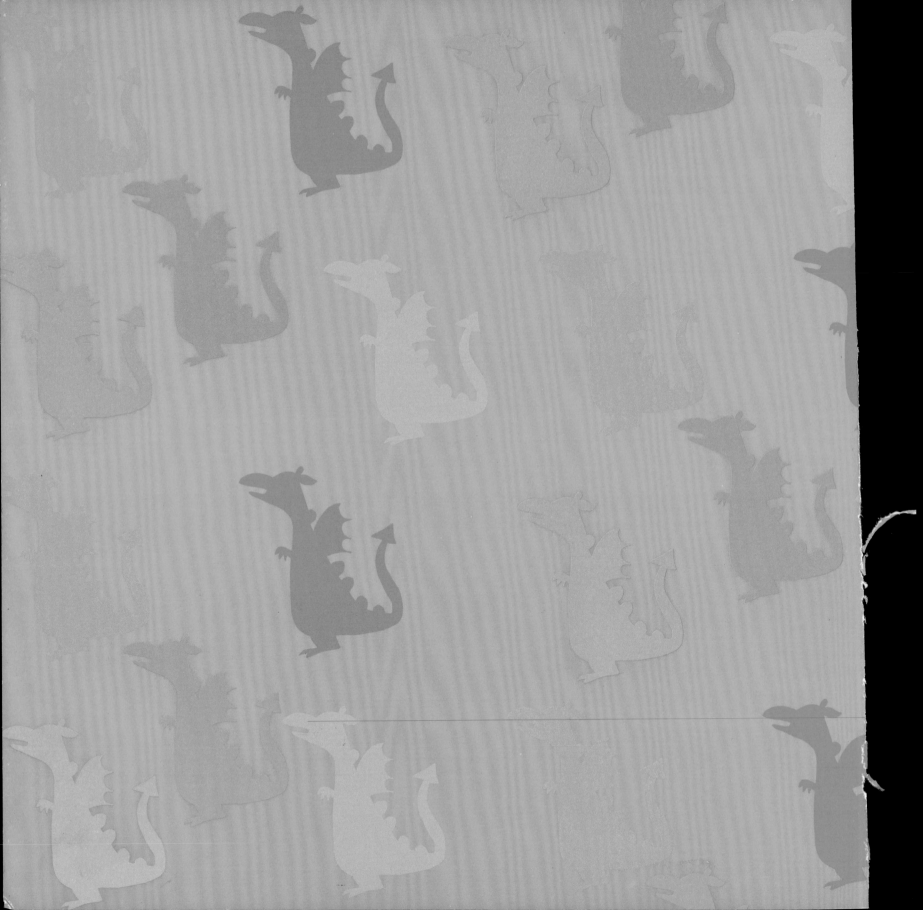